The Box

Dear Jen and Mike,
Merry Xmas!
and many thanks for all your care and friendship
Anthony
xx

Anthony Sauerman

This book is a work of fiction. The characters, dialogue and incidents are either fictitious or are used fictitiously.

A CIP catalogue record of this book is available from the British Library.

Published by Goldcrest Books International Ltd
www.goldcrestbooks.com
publish@goldcrestbooks.com

ISBN: 978-1-913719-88-3

This story is dedicated to my dear friend Yunus.

May he rest in peace.

Chapter 1

Alex

District Six 1968

The bulldozers are coming first thing in the morning. They warned us. Pinned eviction notices on our doors giving us ten days to pack up our belongings and leave. Street after street, home after home, family after family, no stone unturned. I am one of the stubborn ones and am sitting all alone in what remains of my living room, a candle casting shadows flickering across its grimy walls in deference to a bitter southeaster that billows down the slopes of Table Mountain and whistles through the cracks and corners of my rotting windowpanes. On my lap rests the box, clasped tightly between my trembling hands, trembling with the cold, the trepidation, or the anticipation, I am not sure which – everything merges into one nowadays. It is all I have left in the world, my most treasured possession, the one thing that has given me hope and inspiration all these years; a box filled to the brim with memories, a time capsule to transport me back to the most magical days of my life, to that summer of 1905 on the farm.

It is no more than an old cardboard shoe box, a very old one, its sides scuffed and marked, its lid held in place with strips of faded sticky tape brittle with age, like me. It has been my trusty lifelong companion since the very first time, all those years ago, we lay under the leafy canopy of the gigantic old oak trees lining the banks of the dam and kissed and cuddled and shared in each other without a care in the world; in fact, without any understanding of it.[1] It brought me joy and love and strength, more than I could ever have imagined possible. It also ripped my life apart, destroying everything that I ever was and ever had, all in a single moment of madness. Then, in one closing act of truth and understanding, it shepherded me into a corner of the world where I could finally live in peace, this place, my haven of normality. It had power well beyond our wildest dreams.

So long has it been since I last looked inside the box that I have almost forgotten its contents, almost forgotten what you felt like, your athletic body, your smooth, milky-white skin, your almond-

1. In South Africa, 'dam' refers both to a barrier constructed across a river to hold back water as well as to the reservoir or lake that builds up as a consequence.

shaped eyes, your warm smile, punctuated by dimples to drown in. Oh, what exquisite beauty lies locked away within its vaults! I have been in hiding, sheltering away from the pain and emotion that has been building up steadily on the inside of its four sides over the course of my lifetime, almost certain to come spewing out uncontrollably, like lava belching from the depths of the earth, and engulf me. It is not an eruption I have dared to provoke, not one that I have ever felt prepared to face, tempting though this has always been. But the time has now come, I must take one last look, sift through the fragments of our past, caress your face and kiss your lips one last time, and invite you to accompany me on my final journey to the place we could only ever imagine in our wildest dreams. Yes, it is with anticipation that my hands tremble.

The Farm, Summer 1905

He arrived out of the blue, early one crisp, spring morning, on foot, backpack over his shoulder, seeking work on the farm, as if he had been destined for this place. I can remember the moment I first laid eyes on him as if it was only yesterday, as if the world had stopped turning and the frozen frame was etched on the forefront of my mind. Dad, on the other hand, was none too impressed by the intrusion, having a low regard for the Boer generally, and finding this one to be overly confident and cocky, apart from which, he could barely speak English! But mom and I managed to persuade him that the fine specimen of a creature standing before us was indeed worthy of a job and could easily sleep on hay in the barn, safely away from us in the house. We could do with an extra pair of hands around the farm, we argued, and if he did not work out, we could always send him packing.

I am not sure who was more taken by our interloper, mom or me, but it was clear that we both felt an instant attraction towards him, much as we tried to conceal it. She twittered and twirled and flitted and flirted all the way to the barn and back again, like some love-struck schoolgirl, much to his amusement and Dad's irritation, while I adopted a much more furtive approach, quietly catching his eye under the brim of his safari hat. To my absolute astonishment and delight, he returned the look, winked ever so slightly, and enveloped me with a smile that lingers with me to this day. It was life-changing, the moment when each of us knew that we had left an indelible mark on the other and our lives would never be the same again; some unspoken yet crystal-clear thread of communication between us, all without the slightest inkling of what lay ahead.

No one knew where he came from, nor indeed where he was headed, we just knew his name – Johan, or Johannes for formal occasions, like church. The papers he carried betrayed the family name, Fourie, and his date of birth, 1885, making him just twenty years of age at the time. Depending on the angle, or the light, or his mood, or all three, he looked like a teenage boy, or he looked like a mature man, such were the angular features, the bright blond hair, the stubbled jawline set against his calm and tender disposition. He was essentially ageless, possessing a chameleon-like ability to engage with anyone in any environment, male or female, young or old, black or white. He enthralled and captivated everyone who met him, charming yet intimate, engaging yet discreet, humorous yet decorous, a twinkle in his eye that could easily have been mistaken for flirtation, and often was. He harboured no grudge nor prejudice, which automatically stood him apart from everyone around him – the people of our age, who wore race and rank as a badge of honour and kept their distance from anyone who was in any way different, commanding the moral high ground of the day, such as it was. He was, quite frankly, the most beautiful human being I had ever clapped eyes on. And I fell madly in love with him.

It began innocently enough. His weekends were free, so he invited me to go fishing at the dam one Saturday afternoon. Fishing was not really my thing, but who could pass up an invitation like that? Mom prepared a packed lunch for us, and we headed off towards the northern perimeter of the farm where the dam nestles alongside a woodland of tall old oak trees that have borne witness to more human intrigue that I am sure they care to remember. We fished and chatted and ate and laughed and swam and teased and played and finally fell asleep on the soft green grass, the wind rustling gently through the leaves of the trees above us, before we returned home with just one fish apiece, which mom baked for the four of us, eating dinner together at the kitchen table, like a family. It was the most wondrous day of my life, and I prayed it would last forever, it was so heavenly.

We went our separate ways for the night, me to my room and he to his barn. I could barely sleep, the thoughts of the day bouncing around my mind like a troupe of merry minstrels, before eventually drifting off into a deep slumber enveloped by mystical dreams of love, laughter and possibility. By the time I arose and washed for church on Sunday morning, he had set off for the day. Mom was not sure where exactly, but she saw him head out of the gates in a northerly direction and so I drew my own conclusions. My sense of curiosity and adventure took hold, and I told my parents that I was going to the dam for a swim, as I so often did after church. The journey there was not without a sense of trepidation, my stomach churning with butterflies of hope and expectation, of what precisely I knew not; a journey into the unknown, with no turning back.

It was midday by the time I arrived there, the sun was high and hot in the sky, the screeching of crickets and the croaking of frogs ringing in my ears. I scanned the landscape and saw him in the distance emerging from the water in the dam where he had been swimming, wading effortlessly in my direction, completely naked, the sun glistening on his wet skin, illuminating the muscles below, and shimmering tantalisingly on his curly blond hair to form a golden silhouette around his body, like some heavenly creature rising up from the flames below. I stood there mesmerised, taking in the beauty that appeared before me, and I felt a yearning start to burn deep down below in that place where I had only recently begun to take so much pleasure for myself. This was entirely new to me, the whole experience, what I saw and what I felt. I began to panic, petrified that he may look up and catch me gawking, not because I worried that I might be caught, quite the opposite, but because I worried it might ruin the moment, ruin everything, forever, that he would chase me away, and the dream would end in an instant, as they do, never to be recovered. He did look up and he did see me, but to my eternal joy, he never chased me away. Not then. Not ever.

I could never have imagined that something so physical and so visceral could be quite as sensual and emotional as this. And the feeling grew stronger with each encounter, with each tender kiss, each touch of the skin, each exploration of the contour lines marking the curves and the crevices of our bodies. We were in heaven, each taking the other to new heights of passion and ecstasy and love, testing our boundaries and honouring our every wish and whim. He was slow and respectful and delicate, I was impatient, hungry and clumsy, and so we taught each other and found the right way, our way. The feeling of him deep inside me, gently pressing against my inner core, was so overwhelming that I cried out each time, trance-like, with pure elation, which only intensified the craving for more. We found comfort on the straw at night, on the banks of the dam by day, whenever and wherever we were able to escape our surroundings and steal a moment of intimacy. It was utterly exhilarating.

Once, as we lay on the banks of the dam, we gazed up at the blue of the sky peeping through the leaves of the trees and imagined what it would be like to live like this, to spend the rest of our lives in such paradise, eating and sleeping together, in our own house on a hill with a farm and a dam, children running around, growing old together and feeling our final breath on each other's lips. Our eyes glazed over with tears, and we snuggled up closer at the thought, but we both knew, deep down inside, that it would never be possible, that our time together would have to come to an end sometime, somewhere, somehow, but surely it would end. We never talked about it. We did not need to. We both knew, as sure as can be sure. The best we could do was to block out the thought and enjoy our time together for as long as it lasted. It was on this day that we each said to the other, "I love you," and sealed that love with a kiss that I prayed would last forever.

Dad had been a Boer War correspondent with a Cape Town city newspaper, and during his days in the field he developed a passion for photography, with equipment and a skill to match. When the war ended in the autumn of 1902, he brought the camara apparatus home and taught me the art of capturing an image and self-processing it to near perfection, screening out light and sharpening shadows where necessary. I was utterly enthralled and spent hours on end experimenting with different ideas and honing my own skills in the art of photography to the point where I developed a lifelong passion for it and was, a lot later, able to build a career around it. As much the technician behind the lens, I was the player in front of it, creating imaginary scenes and images to gloss up the pain of reality and craft a fanciful world where I could be true to myself, and be free. Where Dad used the device to depict the real-life horrors of the world around him, I used it to escape those around me, my rabbit hole to Alice's White Rabbit. It was enchanting, bordering on the addictive, my fix to the troubles of the day, liberating my soul, if only for the moment. I wanted nothing more than to share in this adventure with Johan, where together we could build our own enchanted garden, our own Mad Hatter's tea party. I suggested to him that we spent a day by the dam with the contraption, capturing images of each other. The idea, I said, was to have something to remember each other by, for posterity, though he was quick to appreciate the theatre of it, and warm to it.

We were joined by Ismael, a young farm hand with whom Johan worked in the fields and with whom we had become close friends. It was frowned upon to fraternise with coloured people generally, let alone with the farm labourers, and I am not sure Ismael's own family would have taken too kindly to him hanging about with us whites either. We therefore had to go about our business with the utmost caution, interacting in private and moving about the farm discreetly. It had never crossed our minds that we should not share our secret dalliance with Ismael, and so we did, openly; and it had never crossed his mind to question it. In this way, he became the third leg of our little tripod, without which Johan and I would have stumbled, and he would have drowned, both in the here and now, and for eternity. Our bond was built on foundations of the forbidden, which only served to strengthen the trust between us and deepen the loyalty we showed towards one another. There can be no better recipe for friendship – thankfully so, considering how vulnerable we three really were, considering the slings and arrows we were to endure in the years to come.

We enjoyed a day of fun and laughter. Johan and I initially posed for the camara separately, then together, with Ismael clicking away to his great delight. I wore pretty dresses, hats and shawls that hung deep in my closet; Johan wore smart suits, silk ties and shoes that we borrowed from Dad; and Ismael wore what he wore every day, a blue overall. As the day wore on and started to heat up, we took off our clothes to swim in the dam and cool down, something that came naturally to the three of us, having spent so much time together and become so close and comfortable with one another's company. We returned to take more images of us three naked, dancing, kissing, cuddling, feigning suggestive positions, all just for the fun of it, one of us always on the camera, the other two taking position up front in an endless stream of cameos and poses. It was sensual, but never sexual; intimate, but never physical; innocent, never naive. When we had used up the whole cartridge of film, we lay down on the grass holding hands and staring up at the sky, feeling exhausted and exhilarated at the same time, oblivious to the troubles that our frivolous day in the sun would cause us. The images we captured on the plates formed ghostly reminders of our everlasting futility, as if we needed them, reinforcing our enduring sense of helplessness and despair. It was Johan who later came up with the idea to entomb the images in the box, as a memorial to our friendship, he said. And so we sealed them away as sure as we sealed our fates, the night before he left the farm.

Johan seldom opened up about his past, and I never asked. He was supremely private and surrounded himself with a protective shield to keep priers at bay. He had various tactics and tricks, but mostly he simply ignored anyone who asked a question that he found too personal, pretending he did not hear or understand it. It gave him an enigma-like quality, which I liked, a mysterious side, an inner sanctum that only he could access. It could be mistaken for the distance that comes with an independent spirit, but I sensed that it was born from some trauma that he struggled to contain and that he needed to control, like shackling a wild animal lest it thrash out at anyone who ventures too near. It was therefore to my great surprise that, late one night, lying breathless on the straw, he started to speak ever so softly, almost indecipherably, about the camp and its horrors. I had no idea what he was talking about. I had never heard about any camps. Mom and Dad never mentioned anything about them at all. Why would they? They wouldn't. They couldn't, it turned out.

His voice grew stronger and louder and angrier, until I had to ask him to quieten down for fear of arousing my parents' suspicion. He calmed down and told me the story from beginning to end. He had been just sixteen when they came, his sister twelve. The farm was burned, the crops destroyed, the animals slaughtered, his mother and grandmother beaten for trying to resist. He felt helpless and responsible, as though he had failed in his manly duty to take care of them, while his pa[2] and oupa[3] were off fighting with the commandos. The camp was filthy, overcrowded, a neglectful, unfriendly place with little food or hygiene, where people died daily from the measles, or starvation, or both, bodies carted off for crude, ungodly burial. He lost them all, ma,[4] ouma[5] and little sis[6] in the camp, pa and oupa on some distant battlefield.

Shame and despair fell upon him, which did not dissipate when they came to liberate him into the care of his dastardly uncle. If anything, the torture

---

2. *Pa* – Afrikaans word for father.
3. *Pa* – Afrikaans word for father.
4. *Ma* – Afrikaans word for mother.
5. *Ouma* – Afrikaans word for grandmother.
6. *Sis* – Afrikaans word for sister.

of the man, his blend of the Bible and the stick, only aggravated matters, until Johan built up the courage to flee his tormentor and seek refuge behind a wall of solitude. For three years, alone in the world, he wandered the land, moving from place to place, stealing a moment's silence, trying to forget, never forgiving, always living in hope of a brighter future. The memory faded, the pain dulled, and light started to shine on his bony face again, at which point God brought him to the farm, to me, to our eternal embrace, a shelter where he could rest his heavy heart and learn to live again, just a little. My place in his journey, infinitesimal though it was at the time, took on a new meaning, one that I could never have imagined and that we could never quite fathom, not then in any event, not yet.

My love for Johan only deepened. He had dropped the veneer and allowed me a glimpse of the inner sanctum, as no one else, the pain and anguish that followed him about like a ghostly shadow, tormented his every waking hour and bedevilled his broken sleep with nightmarish flashbacks and hallucinations. I had too little experience of the world and the people who inhabit it to know whether it was normal to incarcerate and kill off fellow human beings to the extent he described, but intuition told me this was a level of cruelty that belied the teachings of any sermon I had endured and that represented the worst possible sin contemplated by them. The devil had indeed been at work, and my dearest Johan had been sorely damaged as a result. My instinct was to protect and shield, to care and heal, to coddle and cradle, to anoint the scars with aloe oils until they faded into obscurity and oblivion, as if to wipe away the pain from the past and replace it with tender love, well-being and equanimity, as if it was possible to wipe away scars. Naive perhaps, but the instinct was genuine in its intent and determined in its execution, and I devoted my every sinew to his undying salvation, small sacrifice to pay for the time we had together. The weeks rolled into months, which ran into the summer. All the while we bathed on the banks of our dreams and drowned in each other's love for as long as God would allow.

And then, as suddenly as he arrived, he was gone, and it was all over. I woke up one fine morning, expecting to see him slopping out the stables, whistling softly to himself, but to my utter dismay, he was nowhere to be found. I knew this day would come. We both did. There was no note, no goodbye, just an empty void. I felt as though my heart had been wrenched from my body and left out on the banks of the dam to dry out, and I sobbed until it hurt. My parents understood my loss, though not the extent of it, and they could do little to console me. I knew this was final. I knew I would never see him again. His time had come, he had moved on to the next chapter in his life, the next phase in his game of survival. I also knew that it was for the best, that we were destined to be apart, and that the process of patching up our loss had already begun. We had never said as much, but we both knew it.

The Farm, Winter 1912

The phone rings. Mom answers it, accepting the call from exchange.

"It's for you, Alex," she says, "I am not sure who."

"Hello. Yes, it's me. Who? Ismael? Yes, of course I remember. How could I forget? My word, how are you? Where are you?"

The news is not good. They found his body by the side of a road, badly beaten with sticks and stones. They think it was a group of men, but they have no idea who. They will keep investigating, but they are not hopeful of finding the culprits. People are being tight-lipped, closing ranks, not prepared to put themselves on the line for him. You see, he was becoming trouble, hanging out with the wrong people, drinking, fighting, and selling himself, for money, for fun, for women, for men. He picked the wrong one. But it had to happen, there were just too many. The odds stacked against him.

It had been hard on Ismael. They had remained friends and stayed in contact, even lived together for a while. He had watched his closest friend disintegrate before his very eyes, and there was nothing he could do to stop it. What cushion time and distance provided me, no such luxury was afforded to Ismael. His pain was as raw as the cuts on Johan's disfigured face, and as real. And then he told me something that knocked the wind right out of me and literally brought me to my knees in despair and anguish. I asked him where it had happened, thinking it would be some faraway anonymous place, some dark, grim alley in one of the big cities, Cape Town or Johannesburg, but no, no such thing. It had happened no more than five miles from the farm, in the town that was closest to us, a place that I visited frequently and was all too familiar to me. He had never left the area. He had never wanted to. He had always wanted to be close to me, to watch over me, to make sure I was safe. He put his life on hold to take care of me, like some guardian angel. He even visited the farm in the quiet of the night to get small glimpses of me walking in the candlelight from room to room, just to make sure, to check in, to reaffirm his undying love and devotion for me. If only I had known, I could have prevented this from happening, I could have intervened and saved him from himself, from the pain that must have continued to torment him. I could have been his saviour, but instead, grotesquely, I had been the very cause of his downfall. I drove him away from the farm and into the hands of loneliness and helplessness and despair. I utterly failed in my commitment to care for him, as I promised myself I would, as we promised each other. Why hadn't I looked for him, followed up, done something? Why? *Why*? And now it was too late.

Ismael continued speaking. There had been no

funeral, only shame. No one had wanted anything to do with him. Instead, Ismael had persuaded them to cremate Johan's body in the fashion of the Hindu tradition, so that his ashes could be placed in a small urn for safekeeping and eventual burial, when circumstances allowed. Ismael said he planned to move to Cape Town and set up a new life in a neighbourhood called District Six, the fashionable place to be, where people of all colours and religions and orientations lived in peace and harmony side by side, the future, the hope for a new world order. He said he wanted me to join him, he wanted me to leave the farm behind and start a new beginning with him, together. He told me that he loved me, that he always had, and that he wanted to share the rest of his life with me. Yes, Ismael told me all this on the call.

I cannot begin to imagine the sense of loss and loneliness that Ismael felt when he put the receiver down. He had just lost his closest friend in the world in the most terrifying of circumstances and now his offer of a new life had been rejected by the one remaining love of his life. But it had all been too much for me. I felt traumatised, paralysed with fear and wracked with self-hate and pity. Thoughts of taking my life swum around my head, like fish darting madly around a bowl of water. Here I was, failing the two people who were closest to me, the two people who I loved in my life more than anyone else, letting them both down in the most terrible of ways. A feeling of complete helplessness and desolation and failure overwhelmed me. At the age of just twenty-two, my life was about as bleak and empty as anyone could possibly imagine. How would I ever be able to recover from this; how would I ever pull my life together again?

And then it came, his letter, hand-delivered, out of the blue, just like him, a message from the other side, a message of love, my passport to tomorrow. Ismael, dutiful to the end, had arranged for the delivery, on his instructions, in the event of his death:

My dear Alex,

If you are reading this letter, I am gone from the world, and you are not. I am sorry that we did not get the chance to say our last goodbyes, but please understand that I never really left you, nor you me, and so there never would be a last goodbye for us.

Do not feel sad at my passing, please. I am sure I am in a better place now, and besides, I leave this world in the knowledge that I had the good fortune to love the most beautiful person in the world, and what a blessing that has been. You are an angel, the most precious gift I could ever have asked for, the only person who really understood me and made me feel human again. It gives me great strength and peace of mind to know that you are a part of me and will be with me forever. Thank you for your patience and for your understanding. You saved me, truly.

You are the most wonderful person, everything about you, your beauty, your compassion, your strength, but most of all your courage in the face of your reality. Please stay true to yourself, believe in who and what you are, walk tall, with pride and self-confidence. If anyone can, it is you. And be kind to yourself, spoil yourself, follow your dreams, fall in love again and make the most of your life. Do this for me, do it because I love you, because I will always be there by your side, until your final breath, and then on the other side, where we will meet again and live the life we have always dreamt of. I will keep the straw warm for you.

Safeguard the box as a reminder of our time together. I have placed a handful of leaves from the dam on the inside. Our destiny is etched in their veins, that which brought us together and binds us for eternity.

I will love you forever, Johan.

Stellenbosch, Spring 1923

I am living a married life now, we have two children, three and six, the most adorable little things, Chloe and John, the centre of my universe, more than anything I could ever have imagined possible. My love for them is quite overwhelming at times.

I put the past behind me and settled down, took a course on photography, and work like Dad as a photojournalist for the local newspaper. Life is good, we are happy enough. I feel as though I am being true to the words in Johan's letter, making the most of my life. It has not been plain sailing, but we got there in the end.

It is spring, which means we clean the house from top the bottom, sending the kids away for the weekend to be on the farm with my parents. I am in town shopping. I have planned a romantic dinner for us and am feeling excited about it. I am going to make it special.

I return to the house at nightfall, but the lights are not on for some reason, and I sense that something is wrong. I park the car and run inside, calling out for her.

"Shirley! Shirley! Is everything okay? Where are you?"

"Is everything okay? *Okay*? You tell me! What on earth, what is this, hey? What? Tell me!" She is standing in the hallway with the box in her hands. The lid is off.

"What the hell is this, then?! All these pictures. Who are these people? Tell me! Who? A hotnot![7] What are you doing standing naked with a hotnot? And the other one, why are you kissing each other? And you, dressed up in women's clothing! It's disgusting, you are sick, man, I tell you, sick, a bloody pervert!"

I can do nothing to stop her, she has lost all control now, apoplectic with rage.

"And this date here, '05. You were just fifteen years old, for Christ's sake! A child! This is against the law, you know. What were you thinking?"

And then, the final blow.

"The children. What about the children? No, you haven't, have you?! Not the children, please, God, tell me, you have not touched our children. I will kill you. Get out of my house! Get out, now, or I am going to call the police. Now, or I call the police. I never want to see you again, ever, you are disgusting. You will never see the kids again, never, you hear me. I will destroy you if you ever come near us again. How is this possible? Who the hell are you? What are you? Take this disgusting little box out of my house and just go, forever!"

I was not about to explain. How could I? Who am I? What am I? These were not questions I could

7. Hotnot – Derogatory term used at the time to refer to a person of colour, now specifically proscribed in South Africa.

answer, not then, not there, not to her. They were not even questions I was able to answer for myself. But I knew they were questions I needed to resolve at some point in time, if I was ever going to live a normal life, the kind of normal that allowed me to be true to myself. I had made myself believe that Shirley and I lived a "normal" life, married, children, church, lovely home, jobs, friends, family, all the trappings of the typical suburban existence, right down to the swimming pool and pet dog. This was what was expected of me, what my parents had wanted, what people demanded, and what Shirley had dreamt of her whole life. I was lucky to have found her. She was beauty personified, serene, spiritual and grounded, but mostly she had the strength of character to carry the weight of my burden on her shoulders, to look past and over and straight ahead, and to help us forge the family unit that defined our existence and allowed us to walk tall, husband and wife, all without a word of it being exchanged, ever. We both knew there was a greater good to be had, and so long as we remained focused on that goal, all would be well. All, with the exception of one not so minor detail, the inconvenient truth that belied the natural order and threatened to destroy everything we had worked so hard to build. To this day, I still wonder whether this was a path she would have chosen had she known the extent of it. I somehow doubt it.

But with this, with her seeing the contents of

the box, the dreaded genie had been let out of the bottle, changing everything for us, for me, forever, not just the way we had to live, but the way I had to feel, who and what I am. The answers were plainly there for me to see, if only I had opened my eyes, if only I had opened my mind. This was no mere role play, no trivial theatrical gesture, this was the real thing, this was life-changing, this was it. Out of the darkness, like the trigger of a gun, the words in Johan's letter sprang to mind, *stay true to yourself, believe in who and what you are*, and it dawned on me, for the first time, what they really meant, that I had entirely misunderstood what he was trying to convey to me. It is said that God deals the hand, we play the cards. Never before had this adage resonated with me more. I had been dealt the most terrible hand, worse than anyone would, or even could, have imagined, but the time had come to start playing it, exactly as Johan had said in his letter. It became crystal clear what I had to do, and how I had to do it. My whole life suddenly fell into place. I found meaning, and I found freedom, the freedom to be who and what I am, finally. I have the box to thank for that. The box and Johan.

District Six, Autumn 1968

The leaves were falling from the trees when they came, indifferent to our plight. We were forced out, watched over by police, me clutching the box for dear life. There was little more to clutch. This was the end of the road for me, the final chapter. I did not want to start another. It had been good, the best I could have hoped for. Ismael had been an angel. He had taken me in, and we lived together until his passing just a few weeks ago. He couldn't bear to lose his beloved District, and he ended it all, with me by his side, cradling his hand in mine to the end. We were Ismael and Alexis, the slightly odd couple next door, classified coloured, although the wife was a little too white for that. Oh, the joys of apartheid, you had to laugh. And laugh we did, every weekend at The Roxy, me on stage, him running the bar, surrounded by friends and loved ones, we could not have asked for more. You see, we didn't have much, but we were free to be who we were, to be true to ourselves, even if no one else around us was, even though the whole country cried out for freedom. We were ahead of our times, as Johan was ahead of his. We felt blessed in a way, the lucky ones. Yes, it was a tough journey along the way, but we made it in the end, and we knew that was all that mattered. It was what Johan wanted, his enduring legacy to us, his ultimate sacrifice.

I walked out of the house and down the street for the last time, never once looking back, a crisp dried-out oak leaf clasped in my hand. I took a left on Hanover Street and headed up to St Mark's Church where Father Mostert presided. He knew everything. I handed him the box, together with my final will and testament:

> *Inside this box are two sets of ashes. Please place mine with them and bury us together under the oak trees along the wall of the dam.*

I am sure the three of us will be together again.

Chapter 2

Ismael

District Six, Early Autumn 1968

He lies staring at the ceiling, his hand resting gently in hers, shots of morphine wrestling with the pain that sweeps through his body, like an army invading a foreign land. This is his final wish, the last time he will be in control, managing the moment as a playwright directs his play. The corner of his mouth curls into a wry smile as the tragedy of his last act manifests itself in true theatrical style, the Romeo and Juliet of their time. And of their place, this District Six, their sanctuary against the evils of the day. His dearly beloved Alexis by his side, serving him the final order at not inconsiderable personal risk and loss, the ultimate sign of her undying love and devotion to the man who gave her everything she could ever have hoped for, a new lease of life, her fresh start. She understands. Others may not, but she does. There is just too much pain and too much loss, not only of the physical kind, but the mental trauma also of losing their entire world, their home, their neighbourhood, their friends and family, the ultimate act of cruelty, the final twist of the knife. She gazes lovingly at the form that lies limp under the bed covers, knowing there is not long to go and wanting to cherish every last moment, every last beat of the heart, every last breath, to kiss his lips at the very end and send him on his journey into the next world, in the care of heavenly angels. She is calm and content. They had the best of times, and they will meet again soon, very soon.

They do not speak; they do not need to. Words are inadequate and will only disturb the serenity of the moment. Instead, memories flood over them, transporting them back to very beginning and shepherding them through the catalogue of the places and the faces that shaped their lives, like stepping stones across a pond. Or is it the dam? The oak trees rustle in the wind, the grass sways gently back and forth, Johan is running towards them, hat in hand, broad smile on his face, excited to be together again, the farm, the day they frolicked together in front of the one-eyed box that captured their every movement, as if ensnared by a Cyclops and stowed away in their little cardboard sanctuary. Ismael held the box under his arm firmly against his side, as a mother holds her new-born baby, cradling its contents for one last time before handing it over to Alexis for the final act. He had added some bits without her knowing, filling the gaps that kept them apart and augmenting the memories that bound them together. It was only right that she should know the truth of what happened and be given the opportunity to make amends, even at this late stage of her life. He owed it to her. He slowly lifted his arm and pushed the box towards her with a reassuring nod of the head and a smile so warm and familiar that he looked like the young man she met all those years ago on the farm. Not now, he was saying, not yet. When I am gone and when you have the strength and the courage, but before it is too late, take a look inside.

At that moment, a warm sensation of love overcame him and removed the pain that had been gnawing away at his body. He knew it was upon him, but he did not care. He was with the one person in the world who had brought joy and peace into his life and so he felt ready for it. He fixed his eyes on hers one last time, squeezed her hand with all the strength he could muster and let out a gentle sigh that still rings in her head: "I love you." She kissed his lips as she knew she would, and he was gone.

The Farm, Summer 1905

Ismael heard the commotion up at the farmhouse and decided to go up and see what it was all about. The madam was in a state of excitement, running backwards and forwards between the house and the barn, a tall, blond Boer man trotting a few steps behind her, a slightly bemused look on his handsome young face. Kleinbaas[8] Alex was there too, carrying blankets and sheets to the barn, then a bucket and towels and a box full of food, a broad smile on his face. Whoever he was, and wherever he came from, it was clear that the blond one was most welcome at the farm and was here to stay.

Monday morning, sunrise, udders in hand, Ismael looked up to see the Boer enter the cowshed, accompanied by the baas[9] and by kleinbaas Alex. He was surprised to see the kleinbaas – he never usually came to the cowshed, certainly not at this time of the morning, and he had never even so much as acknowledged Ismael, let alone spoken to him.

"This is Johan, boy!" barked the baas. He had stopped calling Ismael *hotnot* following a recent visitation from the local priest, who had received

---

8. *Kleinbaas* – Afrikaans word for small or young boss.

9. *Baas* – Afrikaans word for boss. Baas or boss was the way in which people of colour addressed white men.

an official complaint from the family, the only recourse available to farm labourers in the day. "He is going to be working with you on the farm. You must teach him everything he needs to know so he can be of some use. An extra pair of hands, you know. No mucking about, you hear me! He needs to work, or he goes. Now, get on with it!"

He turned on his heel and disappeared behind the door of the shed, leaving the three young men blinking at each other, the Boer traveller, the son of an English farmer, and the coloured farmhand of Muslim faith. A more diverse trio one could not have imagined, but they were oblivious to it, just three strangers meeting for the first time, yet feeling a strong sense of intrigue and attraction towards one another, fuelled by the suddenness of their encounter, as if ambushed by Eros himself. Unexpected and entirely novel though this sensation was to all three of them, they stood their ground and remained composed, just the sound of beating hearts pounding in their ears like distant drums. In that moment, they transcended the chasms of hatred and prejudice that bedevilled their lineage and tore their country apart, forging their very own paradise island in the shark-infested waters that surrounded them, one that was to become their special place of safety, a sacred haven.

Their journey had begun, shaped as it was by the opportunity to steal time together and secure pockets of freedom for themselves, away from prying eyes and pestering parents. Ismael and Johan worked side by side in the fields as equals, conversing in the local Dutch dialect[10] and getting to know each other as close friends and confidants, pushing the boundaries of affection, but never venturing across them. Johan and Alex became much more intimately acquainted with one another, finding time and space for their dalliance in the bales of straw that littered the barn and on the leafy banks of the dam that baked in the sun. Through Johan, Alex got to know Ismael for the first time, learning to drop the barriers of preconception that had been ingrained in him from the day he was born, as much in relation to people of colour as in relation to the Boer. The freedom was exhilarating.

Through it all, Ismael found himself strangely attracted, physically so, to young Alex, his silky auburn hair, his smooth olive skin, and his almost feline facial features that lent him an androgynous appearance and caught the eye as in the case of any pretty girl, confusing to him though this undoubtedly was. He was aware that an intimacy had developed between the other two, but it somehow felt entirely natural, almost enviable, truly a thing of beauty. He had no reason to question it, nor Johan's part in it, such was Alex's delicate beauty and grace. In fact, he noticed something quite special develop between

10. Afrikaans only became an official language in 1925. Before then, people spoke a form of Dutch dialect on which Afrikaans was based.

them, a love and affection that grew, almost visibly, on a daily basis, as Johan dropped his guard and opened up to Alex, who in turn healed the raw wounds of the Boer's traumatic childhood and nurtured him back to life, as if breaking in wild horses or taming rabid dogs, each step taken with utmost patience and sensitivity, so as not to scare them off. Alex displayed a level of kindness and compassion that Ismael had never before seen in any human being, not even his dear mother, and he marvelled at the effect it had at softening Johan and building his confidence and self-esteem. They were a match made in heaven, made all the more so by the gentle nature of Alex's disposition. Ismael was secretly quite mesmerised by him.

Strong though these feelings towards Alex were, and indeed his desire, Ismael's friendship with Johan acted as an absolute barrier to anything more intimate, with the result that he had to content himself with the formality and distance of friendship, difficult and frustrating though that undeniably was. Thus, throughout the summer of 1905, the three companions lived in perfect harmony with one another, respecting each other's individuality, and providing the mutual love and support needed to foster it. Little were they to know to what extent their fate would be sealed by events following that wondrous day at the dam, the day their paradise island was blown apart by the tectonic plates of the images that betrayed the level of their depravity to the outside world. Little did they care. This was the most glorious time of their lives, and they would cherish each and every moment together for as long as it would last, for as long as God would permit.

A Town Close to the Farm, Winter 1912

Ismael was not surprised that it was him who they contacted. They had seen the two of them drinking together in town and so knew they were acquainted, besides, there was no one else. They needed him to identify the body, more of a formality for their records than anything else, although the body had been badly beaten and disfigured. He was also not too surprised that this had happened at all. Johan had been spiralling out of control for some time and had upset enough people to warrant a level of animosity that was not healthy in a town of the size and morality of theirs, where everyone knew everyone else's business and the Bible reigned supreme. The light had gone out of his handsome, smiling face, his piercing blue eyes had dimmed, his fine athletic frame had started to crumble around him, and he had lost the magnetic aura that so bedazzled them that day he first sauntered onto the farm. He had become tired and lonely, defeated at his tender age. Life had caught up with him, and he started to drown in his own desolation and despair. It was tragic to watch.

Not long after Johan upped and left the farm so suddenly, Ismael followed suit. Alex had gone back into his shell, no doubt from the grief of it, and turned his back on Ismael, perhaps understandably so, Ismael reasoned. They had lost their soulmate, the one thing that transcended their differences and bound them together, and so they reverted to type, back into the world of prejudice and division from which they came. The distance was agonising for Ismael. His family were angry with him for straying from the chosen path and intermingling with people across the divide, and so they took a hard line with him as a form of punishment, believing it to be in his best interests, to bring him to his senses, they said. The day his father found one of the images from their special day – one that he had secretly kept for himself – and took the cane to him, was the day Ismael packed a bag with the few belongings he possessed, kissed his baby sister goodbye, and left the farm for the last time, tears pouring down his face. He was turning his back on everything and everyone he had ever known, and on the one person he loved the most, the lovely Alex, not knowing when he would ever see any of them again.

He knew where he was headed, and found his friend easily enough. They moved in together and made a good enough life for themselves, hustling odd jobs, riding, fishing, charming the young and not so young ladies, swilling beer and lazing about, without a care in the world, or so they feigned. They grew close, even crossing the line of affection on occasion, though more as a natural extension of their friendship than anything else, and always to shelter themselves from the deafening loneliness that haunted them day by day. They kept to themselves, and they were left to themselves. It was as much as they could ask for, under the circumstances. They were content, as content as could be.

One night, as they lay beside one another on their one and only mattress, gazing into the empty darkness, their hands and feet touching ever so lightly, lighter than a feather, just enough to reassure each other of their presence, Johan opened up to Ismael about Alex and why he had left the farm so suddenly. He and Alex had felt a connection from the instant they met, the moment they glanced at each other under the brim of his safari hat and exchanged smiles. It would only be a question of time before something happened. But it was all so thoroughly confusing, so terribly wrong, two men attracted to each other. It simply did not make any sense. It was not that he shunned the male form, just that he had never had any emotional attachment to it, never felt any positive attraction towards menfolk. But this was something entirely different, a feeling he had only ever experienced with women, and only one or two at that. He tried to block the thoughts out of his mind, but they kept flooding back, breaching the barriers of his convention. He tried to keep his distance from Alex, even went out of his way to avoid him, almost as a test to see whether all of this was simply a figment of his imagination; not real at all. He invited Alex fishing to prove a point, to validate that it was no more than friendship that had drawn them together, that there was nothing to be concerned about. That day had gone well, generally. They had had a wonderful time together, two chaps fooling about, getting to know one another, all in the spirit of friendship, all in the gorgeous setting that was the farm. They had passed his test with flying colours. He could relax. And then, as if to shatter the peace, came the day by the dam, the day after, when he caught Alex staring at him through the long grass, and the lid on the true meaning of their friendship was blown wide open, never to be closed again.

Johan struggled to find the words. There was nothing like it. He had never encountered or even heard of the phenomenon before. Alex himself had been unable to elucidate in words how he felt, let alone why. All he knew was that he was not meant to be in the body that God had bestowed upon him. Somewhere along the line, there had been some terrible mistake, he had been assigned the wrong form, or had his brain been surreptitiously switched with someone else's, perhaps as punishment for something he had done in a previous life? Or in this life?

Alex had convinced himself that he could wash it all away if he behaved impeccably, did everything that was asked of him, never let anyone down, loved his parents loyally and unconditionally, worked hard on the farm, completed all his studies, went to church regularly, prayed every day and believed in God the Lord Almighty, self-imposing penance upon himself in the hope it would wipe the slate clean, and he could be normal again. He had no other way of explaining it, and no one to turn to, no information, nothing, just the crazed thoughts swirling around his head. He cried himself to sleep at night in sheer trepidation of what he had become and how he was to live his life. He often contemplated taking his life, but then a new day would dawn, and he would wake feeling re-energised and renewed, almost excited about the adventures that lay ahead for him. You see, Johan explained, Alex harboured a deep secret that made him unique and special, gifted in a way, a secret that stood him apart from everyone else and provided him with a key to happiness and freedom whenever he wanted it, like lighting a candle. The collection of clothing at the back of his wardrobe offered snippets of joy and contentment as he converted his bedroom into a stage in the grand theatre of the universe and donned the characters he so longingly dreamt of, soaring above the mendacity of his existence to be true to himself, if only for a brief moment. He lived for those moments, and he loved them.

Ismael lay in silence listening to Johan's account of their mutual friend, struggling to digest the full implications of what he was hearing and what it meant for himself and for his own feelings towards Alex, his dearly beloved Alex. The pieces of the puzzle started to fall into place to form a picture that was nowhere near as dysfunctional as he had originally believed. Now that he knew, he had to concede that there was something exceptionally beguiling about Alex, a warm, soft, gentle, feminine side to his personality that belied his physical appearance and embodied everything that Ismael found attractive in a woman.

Open-minded as he had always been about Johan's relationship with Alex, it was only now, for the very first time, that he fully understood it, and he realised why Johan felt compelled to leave the farm before it became too problematic, before any harm could befall Alex. It was an act of love, an act of self-sacrifice, protecting Alex from himself and from what could never be. The ramifications were too awful to contemplate, the disapproval, the rejection, an excommunication, flung into the wilderness with nowhere to go and nowhere to hide, abandoned, as he, Johan, himself had been.

Ismael also started to appreciate the sense of pain and loss experienced by Johan in the face of his enduring love for Alex, all those late-night visits to the farm to check in on the one and only person he ever truly cared for and who ever cared for him, making sure he was safe, just wanting to be close by, confirming his presence; small comforts. These trips became his fix, one that drained the life and soul out of him, trip by trip, the addiction taking control and dragging him down ever further into his loneliness and despair. It was all so clear to Ismael, the futility of the situation and his own impotence to do anything about it.

It was the reason why he was not surprised to receive the call and why he felt so calm when identifying the body. This was meant to be. Disfigured though Johan's body was, it was a thing of beauty still, youthful and elegantly proportioned, like a Greek sculpture. He had to resist the temptation to give him one final kiss on the lips, but instead asked to cut off a tuft of his silky golden hair, the tip dipped in crimson red, like a paintbrush capturing their final scene for immortality. A last goodbye whispered into his ear: "Farewell, dear friend. Fear not, I will take good care of her, I swear."

District Six, Summer 1923

Not in his wildest dreams did Ismael believe this day would come. As far as he was concerned, it was over, they were done, if they had ever been in the first place, that was. Alex had so resoundingly rejected him on the telephone call all those years ago that Ismael truly believed he had been erased from his friend's memory, as a wave wipes away love hearts etched into the sand with a stick. It had not been the easiest of calls to make, what with the terrible news of Johan's tragic demise, and knowing the strength and depth of the bond that had existed between him and Alex. The call was also made with the flutter of a heart madly in love, made all the madder by the time and distance that had grown between them, ever hopeful that Alex would reciprocate his expression of love and agree to elope with him. How naive and unrealistic that seemed to Ismael now. Yet it was precisely what he had wanted at the time and what he believed would be the salvation of Alex, his flight to freedom and happiness, to the place where he could be who and what he was, where he could at last be true to himself.

Little did Ismael appreciate quite how deep Alex had buried his past with Johan and hidden himself behind the mantle of normality. Ismael had allowed his own imagination to run wild, fuelled by a cocktail of wishful thinking and best intentions, but entirely devoid of reality. Even Johan's letter, which arrived some days after the call, failed to trigger the epiphany in Alex that Ismael so dearly craved, but instead drove Alex further back into the cage of his lineage, and crucially, of his church. His interpretation of the words in the letter led him in the exact opposite direction and into the arms of an adoring wife, with whom he built a family and settled into suburban life. It dawned on Ismael that perhaps he was the one stuck in the past, that it was he who needed to move on and start a new life. In that sense, the call and its cold ending was the jolt he needed to put his plan into action, to say his final farewells to family and friends and make his big move to the city, to District Six.

And now, having settled into a new life, aeons away from that summer at the farm, the memory of the places and the faces fading into obscurity, there came the knock on the door, faint at first, drowned out by the hustle and the bustle of the street, then a little louder, until it could be heard clearly from the inside. A special delivery, a needy neighbour, the greedy landlord, a hungry street urchin, a friend passing by, the post cart, his favoured money lender, a friendly *bergie*,[11] a troublesome *skollie*,[12] a snooping police officer, he knew not who. It could

11. *Bergie* - A slang term used in the Cape for people who are homeless, originally people who lived on the slopes of Table Mountain (berg).
12. *Skollie* - Slang term used in the Cape for a petty criminal or gangster.

have been any one of them. He opened the door and there before him stood Alex, a slim leather bag in one hand, tailored coat and trilby hat in the other, camera slung over his shoulder, an old cardboard shoebox, sealed with Sellotape, tucked firmly under his arm. He looked as handsome as ever, albeit older, his hair combed to one side, horn-rimmed glasses resting on his aquiline nose, his lily-white skin sweating lightly, nervous as hell, a fish out of water. If you had not known him, you would have said he had the wrong address; the wrong neighbourhood, actually. The likes of him did not often frequent the cobbled streets of this district, not without invitation or good cause. It was clear to anyone who cared to notice that this journey had not been taken lightly, that here was a man travelling from one world into another on a mission that only he fully comprehended. Bold though that had no doubt been, he stood on Ismael's front doorstep as vulnerable as an abandoned baby, hands shaking like leaves and eyes lowered to the ground in meek repose, not knowing how the friend who he had so cruelly betrayed would react to his unannounced arrival. For that is what it was, his arrival.

Ismael always wondered whether people took him for a sucker when he welcomed Alex into his home, indeed into his life, with such wide-open arms, after all the pain and heartache that he had been put through. On a good day, they would have commented on his patience, the patience to hold on so long for this moment to arrive, as he never ceased hoping it would, and on his kindness, the kindness to forgive and forget and to embrace someone in their greatest hour of need. On any other day, the twitching of net curtains, the cacophonous cackle on street corners, strained necks in church pews and tittle-tattle at bar counters betrayed a somewhat different narrative, one that was not quite as generous and understanding. Sticks and stones, it did not bother him in the slightest. He was the happiest man alive, and no one was going to take that away from him, not now, not again. To have Alex by his side was pure joy, a blessing, a true miracle from God.

Ismael listened intently to Alex's account of his long and arduous journey from those heady days at the farm to the cosiness of family life, and its subsequent unravelling in such dramatic fashion, which opened his eyes to the true meaning of the words in Johan's letter – *please stay true to yourself* – and prompted him to make the trip to Cape Town. Ismael understood it all, every twist and turn, every up hill and down dale. There were no shortcuts to be had, no jumping the queue, no spontaneous eloping at the drop of a hat. This had to be done one gruelling step at a time, like a weary army trudging back to base across muddy no man's land. The news of Johan's death – he called it murder – sucked all the life out of Alex and utterly defeated him. He recoiled into himself and ritualistically killed off his alter ego by torching his dresses and disposing of every other adornment, believing them to be the cause of his and Johan's misfortune. Ismael's declaration of love and offer of a new life only made matters worse, driving him into a state of self-hatred and depression, which lasted a period of years. He very nearly threw the box onto the funeral pyre of his self-sacrifice to erase all traces of the sordid affair and its filthy baggage from his memory once and for all and to provide him the fresh start he needed for a new life, wholesome and pure. It had been close, but something held him back, some invisible hand from the past resting on his shoulder and igniting the dimmest of flames flickering softly in the deep recesses of his mind, a faint ray of hope, nebulous yet comforting. The box remained intact and secure, generating the personal strength needed for that faint glimmer of hope to shine on, even if by just a thread.

Alex's parents finally made the bold decision to intervene. It was a risky move with no guarantee of success and every possibility that it would drive him further down and away, but they had watched him spiralling into oblivion for long enough to decide that it was a chance worth taking. Actually, it was just the prompt he needed, the prod that shook him to his senses and encouraged him to pursue his new calling, that of man, son, husband, father, true hunter-gatherer *homo sapiens*, the paterfamilias of his time, loyal and obedient wife by his side, programmed to rear as many children in their litter as they dare, as God would permit.

The church, of course, played a central role in their crusade, bringing Alex and his wife together in the first place and thereafter shepherding them through their lives together. It was prayers at mealtime, at bedtime, at celebrations, ceremonies, commiserations, at every opportunity, buoyed by regular church attendance, Sunday school, Bible readings, priestly visits, village hall fetes, school assemblies, every conceivable civic occasion, and all underpinned by the unyielding teachings of the sacrament imposing guilt and penance on anyone who dared to stray from the path of righteousness. *And forgive us our trespasses, as we forgive them that trespass against us, and lead us not into temptation, but deliver us from evil.* It was the perfect antidote to the debauchery of his youth, just what Alex needed to wash away her past and settle into his new life.

Alex never begrudged his wife's reaction, ever. Any person seeing what she saw in the box, in that age, in those circumstances, would have responded as she had, if not more. Their first impulse would have been the well-being of their children, driven by an instinct to protect them from all evil. It was entirely natural and understandable. He never had a harsh word to say about her, only remorse and concern for her well-being, quite apart from that of the children. She bore the brunt of it, she had to pick up the pieces and pull the happy home together, all on her own. It was to his eternal gratitude that she had not made more of it, shouted it off the rooftops, involved the authorities, told his dear parents, friends, work colleagues and, God forbid, the children, launching ripples of scorn and spite across the pond of their life. She was truly remarkable in this way; stoic and brave, as much in defence of her own dignity as his, no doubt, but extraordinary, nonetheless. Thankfully, she did not want the whole family dragged through the mire and so she acted with utmost discretion and guile. Hardest of all, that question: where is Dad? How to look the children in the eye and provide an explanation that was not only plausible, but did not scar them for life in the belief that their father had completely abandoned them? It was difficult, no doubt, but they were young, gullibly so, and over time the memory faded, and the loss softened. Never fully, though – the scars never heal.

Thus it was that Ismael welcomed Alex into his home, bridging the gap of the eighteen years since they first met and wiping clean the slate of loss and pain that characterised it, the living embodiment of the words in Johan's letter: *be kind to yourself, spoil yourself, follow your dreams, fall in love again and make the most of your life*. His gift.

Chapter 3

John

Stellenbosch, 1948

I have long since reconciled myself to the fact that for some reason, seemingly too complicated and difficult to explain, my father abandoned the family when I was a child of no more than six years old, and he never felt able to contact us again. It was a bitter pill to swallow, primarily because it was such a dark mystery, but also because Chloe and I had to live with an enduring sense of loss and abandonment. What could possibly have compelled him to desert his wife and children and start an entirely new life somewhere else without us? If it was an affair, a mental breakdown, jail time, conscription into some war, a job opportunity oversees, anything, why not just tell us and be done with it? We would have taken the explanation on board and adjusted ourselves to our new norm, as children do. Did it not aggravate the whole affair by maintaining a permanent cloak of secrecy over it?

From the age that we were old enough to develop these thoughts, Chloe and I would sit in the dark after lights-out pondering every last possible explanation, theorising what could have become of the man, and why Mom point-blank blocked any discussion on the topic. We had tried on several occasions to ask her, but we could see that it only led to more distress and anxiety, and so we never pursued it any further. She was a delicate soul, who carried the weight of the world on her shoulders, and so the least we could do was lighten her load as best we could by avoiding the question of who and where our true father was. No, this was a riddle we had to solve for ourselves, in our own time, in our own way. In truth, there was no great urgency to it. We had had a good enough childhood, a caring home environment, the perfect schooling, all the love and security that any child could possibly hope for, all things considered. We were, to all intents and purposes, well-adjusted kids, who just got on with their lives as effectively as any other. That felt enough.

Until one day, on my twenty-first birthday, in the year 1938, when I had occasion to see my birth certificate for the very first time. I was clearly not meant to see it, but I spotted an opening and seized the moment. We were at the lawyer's office in town, Mom wanted to transfer the ownership of some shares she had bought over the years to me, a coming-of-age gift, she said, and we were required to sign the necessary transfer documents before a notary public. The lawyer's assistant had casually left the file open on her desk and there, lying at the very top of it, was the official document, as clear as day: Republic of South Africa Abridged Birth Certificate, Surname: Scott, First names in full: Johannes Alexander. My full name, Johannes Alexander Scott. How was this even possible? To the best of my recollection, I had only ever been known as John, John Alexander Scott, Alexander being the name of my long-lost father. That much I knew, but never Johannes, not even Johan. The name was entirely new to me. What made it all the more unusual was bestowing an Afrikaans name upon a child born into an English-speaking family. It was unheard of. Why would you? You wouldn't, which is presumably why the family chose to ignore the name and call me by its English equivalent, John. But why? Was there a Johannes? Who was he? Why had I never been told about this before? Why had it been swept under the carpet? So many unanswered questions.

I felt like I had stumbled upon something significant, but I had absolutely no clue what it could be, or where to start looking, who even to ask. This was too big for me to discuss with Chloe at her age; besides, she was just about to write her final school exams, and this was the very last thing she needed on her plate right now. Mom would not have taken well to this line of questioning, I was sure. In fact, thinking about it, she must have known why I had been given the name Johan in the first place, and why it had subsequently been changed. She may even have done it herself and been hiding it from me my whole life. But why on earth? To protect someone? Me perhaps? To hide something from the past, something about our family lineage?

Perhaps it was a lot simpler than that. Perhaps it had been an administrative error in the births' registry office, which my parents chose to ignore, preferring me to have an English name, nothing more. They may have believed that I would be held back in life, that people would question my background, who and what I really am – a Brit or a Boer? What could be worse than being a Boer nowadays, hey? It could be anything, literally, but I needed to find out, somehow, somewhere, and then it dawned on me – the only people I knew who had any connection with the family history, who had been around when I was born and who had known my father only too well, were his parents, Gran and Grandad, on the farm.

We used the visit the farm regularly before Dad left us, every other week or so. Certainly, every month. I had been a very young child and so could not recall much detail from those days, but I do remember the farm being a place of fun and laughter, a place where we children could play freely outside without our parents having to worry where we were or what we were up to. I also remember it being a place of particular joy for my father. He used to look forward to our visits for days in advance and his whole demeanour somehow changed when we got there. He became more relaxed and light-hearted, full of energy and laughter, enough even for me to notice at my tender age. It was clear that he had many happy memories about his upbringing on the farm and that these visits totally rejuvenated him in a way that little else did.

I specifically remember him once taking me on a long walk to the other side of the farm, where there was a dam surrounded by beautiful old oak trees and where we ran about in the long grass, the two of us screaming and shouting into the wind, free as birds. I had never witnessed him like this before, or since. It was wonderful to see. And then we lay down on the banks of the dam looking up at the blue sky and he told me something that has stuck in my mind ever since. Taking my hand in his, his voice trembling slightly with emotion, he told me that this was the place where Chloe and I first touched down and came into the world, where God first started to mould us into the beautiful human beings we were today. He told me that this was a sacred place and that it had been dedicated to the two of us, and to no one else. He said it would protect us throughout our lives, whatever happened around us.

I mentioned all of this to Chloe in our midnight chats after he disappeared, but she had been too young to notice any change in him at the time, or to speculate why this could even have been the case. We just put it down to the magical aura of our grandparents, who were two of the most wonderful people you could imagine, salt-of-the-earth, coupled with the magnificent setting of the farm in which Dad grew up. As for the sacred place, the grassy bank of the dam, we could only guess that it was where one or both of us had been conceived, a special spot that Mom and Dad had picked out, where they could be private and intimate, a place of particular meaning to them. It really should have been dedicated to her, but such was the generosity of the man that he graciously bestowed it upon us. His lasting legacy to us. What a blessing. Yet, a blessing that we were required to bottle up and place on the mantlepiece of our minds, because my trip to the dam that day was the first and last time either Chloe or I ever visited the sacred place that he so lovingly conferred on us. In fact, it was the last time either of us ever visited the farm as children. Not long after this trip he disappeared from our lives forever, and with him, our visits to the farm. Mom would have nothing more to do with the place.

They sat next to each other, holding hands, on the edge of their floral sofa, nervous and fidgety, not knowing how to answer my question. I had ambushed them, unfairly, firstly arriving at the farm unannounced and secondly diving straight into the topic the moment they had laid out the tea tray, adorned with home-made biscuits and scones. Not my finest hour, I would say, reflecting on it, not the greatest display of respect and empathy for the two people in the world who had given me nothing other than their love and affection and who were undoubtedly innocent bystanders to whatever it was that was going on. It was clear that they knew something but were reluctant to share the information with me – whether out of concern for my well-being or out of a desire to protect someone else; it was hard to say. They sat paralysed with fear, like rabbits in the headlights. It was agonising to watch. I slumped back in my chair, staring at the empty space between us, regretting that I had made the trip at all and placed them in such a compromising position. The silence was deafening and seemingly endless, before slowly, softly, soothingly, checking in with each other, they started to speak, until the words started to tumble out of their mouths, and they were unable to stop.

They told me all about the summer of 1905. All that they knew, that is. Well, all that they told me they knew. On the face of it, there was nothing remarkable to it – a young Afrikaner man looking for work on the farm, my father, an only child, befriending him, the two of them developing a close friendship, spending all of their free time together, trips down to the dam to swim off the heat of the day. And Ismael, a young farmhand, who always helped them out with chores and accompanied them wherever they went. A day spent together taking images on Grandad's state-of-the-art camera, much fun and much laughter, all going well until one day, completely unexpectedly, the Afrikaner upped and left and was never to be seen again. No one knew where he went or what he did thereafter. Years later, there was a call, and my father was told that the man had died; in fact, that he had been killed in quite tragic circumstances, the details of which escaped them, conveniently. And that was the last they ever heard of him, and the last my father ever spoke of him. That was it, that was everything there was to know. Oh yes, one more thing. They both looked up at me as if to check that I was ready. The Afrikaner's name was Johan.

Johan, or Johannes, no doubt. The second time that the name had cropped up in as many weeks. Surreal, I think they call it, to be learning about your own true name, a name that was subsequently taken away from you, and your namesake, a person you had never met or even heard of before, all at the same time; and the namesake, such a close companion to your father – the man who abandoned you as a child and disappeared into thin air – and eventually murdered in such terrible circumstances, never to be heard of again. Surreal, no question. There had to be more, there just had to be.

A million questions sprang to mind, but I had

put the two of them through enough for one day. I had been through enough for one day, for that matter. This was more than any person could digest in one sitting. I needed time to take it all in, for the implications of what I had just heard to percolate through my conscious self. I needed to get home and think things over.

As I was making myself ready to leave, Gran took hold of both my hands in hers and looked me straight in the eyes, tears streaming down her face.

"Don't be angry with him," she said, "he was a good man, a wonderful boy, the best son I could have wished for. We loved him dearly." With that, she pulled an old, curled-up photograph out of her pocket, the one remaining memento she had left of her beloved son, and said: "Please, take this. He would want you to have it."

First, the birth certificate, now this, a photograph, defining objects in my life, beyond my wildest imagination, the first two stepping stones of a journey into the unknown. It was unnerving, not knowing where this would lead me and how it would end. My trip to the farm had answered one part of the riddle – whether there was ever anyone called Johan and who he might be – but it also opened up the proverbial Pandora's box and told me nothing about my father, why he had left us so suddenly, where he could be today, and why he chose to name me after his friend. If nothing else, he and this Johan character had something in common, feeling able to walk out of people's lives at the drop of a hat, never to be seen again. Perhaps Dad had felt a sense of abandonment and betrayal by his friend, and carried those feelings with him into adulthood, never able to process them sufficiently to manage his own actions. It remained a total mystery.

I sat staring at the photograph for ages. Two young men standing side by side in three-piece suits, arms tightly interlocked at the elbows, happy smiles on their faces, chests proudly puffed out, against a backdrop of tall oak trees, the self-same trees that enveloped my father and I that day at the dam. Looking at the picture, you would say these were the best of friends, thoroughly at ease in each other's company. The one was clearly Dad, the other, a much taller man, I knew to be Johan by the notation that had been scrawled in pencil on the back of the photograph: *me and Johan, in our Sunday best*. So, there he was, this Johan character, who seemed to have played such an important role in Dad's life, and now mine. Nice to meet you, sir, delighted to make your acquaintance. Now, please, just tell me, who the hell you are!

Another thought came to me, one that turned out to be a critical piece of the jigsaw puzzle, albeit years later. Two people in the picture, out in front of the camera, there must have been a third, the person taking the picture, standing behind the camera. Gran and Grandad mentioned a farmhand by the name of Ismael, who had always been around and helped them with everything, like some sort of Man Friday. He must have been the photographer, and, judging by their broad smiles and relaxed pose, they must have been very comfortable in his company, opening themselves up to him in an affectionate and trusting way, possibly even as a friend, as equals. This would have been unusual, but not unheard of, particularly in rural settings where people worked shoulder to shoulder farming the land, as they presumably had. I could well imagine the three of them forming a friendship in a place like the farm, cut off from the hustle and bustle, the phobias and prejudices of life outside, a safe haven where they could just be free to interact with one another as though it was completely normal, without a care in the world. If the imaginary world I constructed for them was even partly accurate, it must have been a magical place, how it should be, a blueprint for a society of the future. I envied them their honesty and freedom, and wished I could have been a fly on that camera, if only for a moment.

And that is where the trail ended, at least where I ended it, for the time being. I had gathered enough information to answer some important questions for myself and to form an impression of the world inhabited by my father, which was, quite frankly, somewhat idealistic and romantic, the way I saw it. My life lurched forward at pace. I studied law at the University of Stellenbosch, where I met my lovely wife-to-be, Wendy, and enjoyed our student lives to the full. We married soon after and had three children of our own. My sister, Chloe, went to Johannesburg to study photography, following in the footsteps of Dad and Grandad before her. She also married and brought two lovely children into the world. Life was good, if you ignored the political poison swirling around us at the time. If you were able to ignore it, that is, with all the hatred and division that spewed across the country. We closed ourselves off from it, safely secluded in our white suburban bubble, and we did our best to shelter the children from the worst of it, sending them to private schools. In that way, in blissful ignorance, life was as good as we ever could have hoped for ourselves.

And then, all of a sudden, it wasn't. The year 1948 witnessed the unexpected win of the Afrikaner National Party in the *swart gevaar*[13] election, heralding the beginning of the nightmare that was to become apartheid, the enforced separation of our people based on the formal classification of our race. It also witnessed the first signs of Mom's cancer, which by then had tragically spread through her body, leaving her with just months to live. As with so much of her life, she was stoic to the end, never once complaining, never making demands,

13. *swart gevaar* means 'black peril' in Afrikaans and was the basis on which the National Party campaigned in the 1948 election.

always putting others first, not wanting her rapid decline to cause anyone undue distress. Following my father's departure, she had borne the full burden of caring for the family, but now it had caught up with her, and she slipped away peacefully in her sleep one night, leaving a legacy of love and caring for her two children and five grandchildren, the most beautiful soul. After the funeral, Chloe and I privately arranged for a memorial stone to be placed on the banks of the dam under the canopy of the oak trees that she would have loved so dearly, with the inscription:

For our dear mother, Shirley, a sacred place
to rest in peace, with all our love,
yours forever A, C *and* J.

I was back in the lawyer's office, the same office where I spotted my birth certificate all those years before, this time to help out with the winding up of Mom's estate. She had left an envelope stuffed to the brim with old papers and documents, "The important ones," she said: her will, title deeds to the house in Stellenbosch, insurance certificates, bank statements, car registration papers, her marriage certificate with Dad, and some correspondence – a tied-up bundle of old letters, some from the very early days, some to and from Dad when they were courting, exactly as you would expect between two young lovebirds, extremely touching and all the more poignant, knowing how it had ended between them. If anything, it just added to the mystery of it, feeling the depth of the love that existed between them at that time.

One letter nearly escaped my attention, tucked away on the inside of one of the legal documents, as if it had been carefully hidden, addressed to Mom, from Dad, at an address in District Six of all places, dated 1 August 1923, no more than six months after his departure.

My dear Shirley,

I hope and pray that this letter finds you in good health.

I cannot begin to imagine the pain that I have put you through and I apologise unreservedly for everything that I have done, and am. I know you will never forget, but I do hope you will find it in your heart to forgive me, if not now, one day. I truly loved you with all my heart and never meant to hurt you or the children. You were my entire world and will remain with me in my heart until my dying day.

I can imagine that I may never see you or the children again, and I can understand why this must be so. This is painful for me, too, believe me. As a small gesture of the gratitude and appreciation for everything that you have done for me, and continue to do for the children, I will be making regular monthly payments into your bank account, as much as I can possibly afford, which will not be much to start with, I am afraid. I ask that you please accept these and use them as needed, with one special request that you use a portion of the proceeds to purchase shares for the children, to be granted to them when they each turn twenty-one to help them get a start in life. This will be the very least I can do for them, and hope it will go some way towards alleviating the pain I have inflicted on them. It is my only wish, and our last act together.

Please take good care of yourself, and make a new life for yourself. I wish you all the happiness and love in the world.

With all my love, Alex.

Such a letter should never have to be written. It was as distressing to read now as it must have been to write or to receive. A cocktail of love and pain and loss, seeking forgiveness and redemption for some irreconcilable sin, so caring and sensitive, the utter desolation and tragedy of the fate that befell them, with the genuine concern for the well-being of Chloe and myself. The symbolism of that trip to the lawyer's office on my twenty-first birthday to take ownership of the shares came crashing down on me. The fulfilment of a commitment made to soften our pain, but more remarkably, of the tacit pact that endured between my parents to honour that commitment jointly over a period of fifteen years, notwithstanding whatever it was that came between them. Any misgivings that I may have harboured were quickly dispelled when I saw the credit entries on the monthly bank statements in the name of A. Scott. It was all there, the affirmation of their parental love and support for Chloe and me, the one thing we had been missing all our lives, the one thing Mom had been too afraid to share with us.

As a parent myself, I could not begin to imagine the dread they must both have felt at letting down their children and therefore the need to do everything in their power to make amends, as Mom surely did, so courageously and so consistently. He had his part to play in this, I can now see, even if it manifested itself in something material, enabling Chloe and me to attend the best schools and universities available, and giving us the kick-start to purchase our first homes. How he must have sacrificed his life to make all of this possible for us, how he must have despaired at not being able to share in it, to watch us grow into adults. One more stepping stone to navigate, more pieces of the jigsaw puzzle tumbling into place, yet leaving gaping holes where unanswered questions emerge anew, like ghosts in the night. How is it possible that it could have led to this? I was as far away from the answer to this question as I was at the age of six, and I knew what I had to do.

District Six, 1953

I had heard of District Six, but I had never visited the place. In fact, no one I knew had ever visited it. It was a place people like us never went. They said it was a slum that was infested with disease and depravity and danger, a place that needed to be cleaned up, but we all knew what they meant. It was a microcosm of the exact world they were trying to eradicate, where people of all creeds and colours, and now, classifications, mingled happily amongst one another: Jews, Muslims, Christians, whites, blacks, coloureds and every other conceivable category of person. This was intolerable to the governing classes, leaving a dark cloud hanging perpetually over its very existence.

All I had was an address, and an instinct that Dad would have continued his passion and worked as a photojournalist for one of the daily newspapers, as he had done before in Stellenbosch. I scoured all the newspapers I could get my hands on, checking for references of photographers against the pictures, starting with the mainstream broadsheets and working my way down the list. I was about to give up when my eye caught the initials AS beneath a photograph that appeared in a lesser-known weekly journal by the name of *The Torch*, which acted as the official newspaper for the so-called Non-

European Unity Movement. An anti-apartheid political mouthpiece, no doubt, unlikely to be up his street, but my last port of call before building up the courage to visit the address in District Six in person.

The phone was answered almost immediately.

"Hello, Gloria speaking, how can I help you?" The click-clack of typewriters was audible in the background.

"Oh, yes, hello, how are you?" My polite best. "I hope you can help me. I am looking for someone, who I think may work for your newspaper."

I could sense her hesitation. It would have been unusual for them to be receiving a call like this from a person speaking like me at a time when so many of their journalists and editors were the subject of harassment and intimidation on the part of the authorities. It was hard for them to trust anyone.

"Who is this speaking?" she wanted to know.

"My name is John Scott and I am looking for my father, Alex Scott. I think he may be a photographer with your newspaper."

There was a silence at the other end of the phone, then I heard muffled voices in the background, followed by stifled giggles.

"No, sorry, luvvy, there is no Alex Scott here." Her tone told me that she wanted to end the call right there.

"But wait, please wait," I pleaded. "One of your photographs has the initials AS against it, and I was thinking, I was hoping, it might be him."

Another silence, some more muffled voices, then another voice, this time a man.

"Hello, sir, this is Trevor Jacobs, assistant editor, speaking. Yes, we do have a photographer working for us with the initials AS, but the name is not Alex Scott. Her name is Alexis Scott."

Alexis Scott! It could not be possible. I must have had the wrong person. But this was way too much of a coincidence – Alex, Alexis, the same surname, doing the same job, a photojournalist, it just seemed too much of an accident.

"Are you sure?" I asked in disbelief.

"Of course I am sure," he said emphatically. "She was in the office yesterday, in the flesh, as sure as I am speaking to you on the phone now. You are her son, you say? Well, I will tell her you called, but she is out of town for a few days on an assignment, so you will need to be patient, and understanding. Give me your full name and telephone number, and I will ask her to call you back."

I panicked. I had no idea what was going on, or what to do. I had heard enough and slammed the receiver down. How could this be possible – Alexis Scott, a woman? There had to be a mistake. But the same surname! This surely could not be a coincidence. I instantly regretted ending the call. How could I? What was I thinking? I wanted to call back, but they would have thought I was crazy, one of the many nutters I am sure they encountered all the time. No, I couldn't call back, not after I had been so rude. But it just didn't make any sense.

Suddenly, as if ambushed, two words in Dad's letter to Mom jumped out at me, much as I had ignored them at the time: *and am*. They had made no sense to me, added onto the end of the sentence like that, left dangling in limbo on a mountain ledge. I *apologise unreservedly for everything that I have done, and am*. Why would it be necessary to apologise to your wife for who you are? I felt as though I was getting closer to the truth, but it was all just too implausible for me to be jumping to conclusions. My father, living the life of a woman? Surely it was not possible. Or was it? There were still so many unanswered questions, so many missing pieces of information, seemingly driven by deliberate concealment rather than any lack of knowledge, which only served to deepen the mystery and strengthen my resolve to get to the bottom of it all. I had come this far, cobbled together so many of the missing pieces, I had to see it through to the end, for my own peace of mind at least, but for all of us, to bury the matter once and for all. There was one more thing that I needed to do. I had the address – 5 Dover Street. I must visit the place in person and see what was going on for myself.

Dover Street runs perpendicular to Table Mountain, its majestic form towering over the rooftops of the George Goulding High School in Plymouth Road when looking up the street, the newly reclaimed Table Bay harbour visible far below when looking down. Small children play makeshift games up and down the cobbled roadway, rusty cars are parked neatly behind one another to one side, some balanced precariously on piles on bricks in place of pilfered wheels. Old newspapers pirouette crazily about in the billowing southeaster wind before settling down into the corners of alleyway, where piles of litter collect. Bright sunlight bounces off the cobblestones, only to reflect onto the crumbling weather-beaten walls of the drab terraced houses, adorned with tall, stately sash windows and beautifully crafted cast-iron Broekie Lace[14] balcony trimmings, relics of their former glory.

The little houses look much of a muchness and so I had to scan the numbers closely to find my way to number 5, at the Hanover Street end, as closely as I suspect their occupants scanned me in return. Poised to knock on the door, I had so many thoughts flying about my head that it was hard to focus on anything at all, even to remember why I was there in the first place. An address on a letter, dated thirty years ago, of a place that the person who used to be my father may have lived at the time, in a world that could well have been on another planet, and me, the call with the newspaper editor fresh on my mind, on a quest to find answers to questions that had eluded me for the full thirty-six years of my life. I had the small comfort of knowing that whoever

14. Broekie Lace – Victorian cast-iron lattice trellis work resembling the lace edgings on women's underwear (broekies = panties).

answered the door, it would not be Alexis Scott, at least according to the voice on the phone who had told me she was out of town for a few days.

A coloured man, with smooth skin and fine, handsome features for someone of his mature age, and elegantly dressed in casual wear, opened the door to greet me. Speaking ever so softly, he uttered words befitting the Good Samaritan: "You must be lost. Come inside, please. Follow me, this way."

I was taken completely off guard and found myself being swept into the entrance hall of the little house and down the corridor towards the living room, where another man, younger and stockier than the first, a dog collar betraying his calling, sat in an armchair. The priest stood up, walked over to me and held out his hand, formal, yet friendly.

"Good afternoon, I am Father Mostert, and this is Mr Abrahams, Mr Ismael Abrahams. How very nice to meet you. How can we help you?" I knew I was in the right place.

The room was small but homely, framed pictures on the walls, comfortable sofas and armchairs, a colourful rug stretched out across its oak floorboards, a simple art deco chandelier dangling from the centre of the ceiling, casting dim shadows across its wallpapered walls. Some family photographs on a sideboard, one all too familiar, of Chloe and me standing side by side outside the house in Stellenbosch. They instantly saw my reaction, looked at each other, smiled and nodded knowingly. They knew it was me, whether from the way I flinched at the portrait or from my genealogical resemblance to Dad, they knew. It was as if they had been waiting for this moment and were prepared for it, although their eyes betrayed the sense of excitement and anticipation they both must have felt now that it had finally arrived.

I need not have done so, but I introduced myself in return, instinctively: "My name is John Scott. Johan." I added, and I held out my hand to shake theirs, connecting the universe of time and space in that single gesture. I felt strangely at home.

We talked for hours and hours, late into the night, stopping only to eat some food and drink some tea. There was so much to tell on both sides, it was hard to know where to start or when to end. They both appreciated the sensitivity of the information they were destined to divulge to me. They had clearly discussed this day many times before, and planned it carefully. Little did they know that I had had the benefit of reading Dad's letter to Mom, and so there was no need to assure me of the love and devotion that lay behind it, yet they nonetheless reiterated it all, time and time again, as if there was nothing more important, his love for Chloe and me. Yet, no matter how it was dressed up, no matter what path the discussion took, we three knew it would all come down to the single question of Alexis, of who and what she was. I told them about the conversation I had had with the deputy editor of the newspaper, about the two little words in Dad's letter to Mom, about the mystery that surrounded his departure all those years ago, and about my increasing sense that somehow Dad was no longer the person he was before, that he was living a completely different life as someone entirely different, going by the name of Alexis. It helped me to say all of this out loud to them, as much as it helped to break the ice for them to tell me everything that had happened, and why.

Dad had been roughly my age, just a few years younger, when he knocked on Ismael's front door in the summer of 1923. It was why Ismael knew exactly who I was the moment he opened the front door to me – we were chips off the old block, he told me. He had a feeling of déjà vu. He had welcomed Dad into the house as he welcomed me, with open arms, and thus started a new chapter in their lives together, in District Six. It was not without its challenges, considering the number of adjustments they needed to make to forge a life together, racial, social, even religious. The District was a world away from anything that Dad had ever known and so it took him time, a number of years, to settle down with a new job, a different church, a fresh circle of friends and most importantly, with Ismael. Dad had not seen him since he followed Johan away from the farm in 1905 and had only spoken to him the once, on that fateful telephone call in 1912. Even the call had been somewhat of a blur for Dad, what with the tragic news about

Johan and the declaration of love from someone he had effectively blocked out of his mind, someone who sat on the other side of the racial divide. That pronouncement only served to bury poor Ismael even deeper into Dad's past, without so much as a thought about Ismael's true feelings for him. It had only been when Mom threw him out that Dad started to see the world in a new light, as it was meant to be, the true meaning of Johan's letter, the nature of his own being, and the love and devotion that Ismael displayed to him in the face of his total rejection, accepting dad unconditionally for who and what he was, those unanswered questions.

This had clearly been the greatest adjustment of all, the moment Dad informed Ismael that he would no longer be Alex, but Alexis, and that he wished to spend the rest of his life living as such. It transcended everything else and fundamentally changed every aspect of their lives as individuals and as a couple. In some sense, it was easier for Dad, having completely turned his back on his past life and entered an entirely new one, in a totally different place, where there were no reference points, only the muffled murmurings of anonymous chortles, jibes and abuse from utter strangers – *moffie*,[15] Tupperware *poesie*,[16] *meisie*[17] and more. For Ismael, it was not so much a case of sticks and

15. *Moffie* – Derogatory Afrikaans word for someone who is gay or a cross dresser, akin to faggot.
16. Poesie – Derogatory Afrikaans word for vagina, akin to pussy.
17. *Meisie* - Afrikaans word for young girl.

stones – the words hurt a little more, having lived in the neighbourhood for so long and become such a familiar figure about it. But what friends and connections he lost he more than gained as the two of them settled into their new norm, Ismael and Alexis, the unusual, if not adoring couple on Dover Street. The Roxy became the centre of their social world, where Ismael took command of the bar and Alexis took command of the stage, entertaining guests from all quarters of the city every Saturday night with a cabaret show to match Paris's Moulin Rouge. Or so it was written in the local papers, with cuttings to prove it. They had found their place, made peace with the world and lived each day as though it was their last.

When just about everything had been said, every question asked, Ismael stood up, went to the bedroom at the back of the house and returned with an old cardboard shoebox, which he placed on my lap. He could see that I was struggling with the avalanche of information they had shared with me, and with that one piece of information in particular – who Alexis was. The more and more they tried to explain the position, the more questions I asked and the cloudier everything became. It was just so unnatural. I had never encountered anything like it before; never even heard of it. I had always considered myself to be open-minded and liberal in my views, even progressive, according to my wife and our circle of friends, who cautioned me against drawing too much attention to myself on the political front. But I had to concede, we lived in a strait-laced, conservative social cocoon that guarded against anything too different and threatening, and was unlikely to encounter, let alone tolerate, anything like this. It was one thing to be homosexual – although we did not actually know any – but I really struggled with the idea that a person could be born into the wrong body and choose to spend the rest of their life as the opposite sex. And my father, at that! The man who married my mother and raised two children, living a completely normal life with friends, family, a member of the local golf club, the church, a respectable job at the newspaper, everything going for him, and then completely destroying his life and ... and – I had to choose my words carefully so as not to offend my two hosts – resorting to this. It just did not make any sense.

Father Mostert and Ismael looked at each other and nodded in silent agreement. They could not have me walk out the door in such a confused and disheartened state of mind, with no way finding any more answers, and expect me to return home and get on with my life as if nothing had happened. They had started this journey with me, they needed to end it. They owed me that much, they felt.

Ismael spoke: "Take this box back to your hotel with you and spend as much time as you want, as much time as you need, going through its contents.

It is a snapshot of your father's life, his other life, the life you have never known. It will fill in some of the missing gaps and give you a first-hand impression of the life he has had and has chosen to live. I hope and pray that it will help you to understand and accept him for who he has become, for who he is." And then he added, "But please bring it back. It holds special memories for him; for both of us, in fact. It goes way back to our days on the farm, when we first met, when we were just innocent kids playing around together without the faintest idea what life had in store for us, and it has followed us through our lives ever since, collecting little artefacts and mementos along the way, not all of them that pleasant I am afraid, but the bits and pieces that bind us together and carried us to where we are today. It allows us to travel back into the past whenever we need some reassurance, and it gives us the strength and hope we need to face the future, our little safe haven. Please, please, bring it back."

Back at the hotel, I opened the box and sifted carefully through its contents. A letter from Johan, addressed to *My dear Alex*, a love letter, no question, and clear in its message, with the hindsight being bestowed upon me. A lock of hair – his, Johan – bright blond, dark coagulated blood smeared across the tip. A small, sealed ampule, presumably containing the ashes of him that Ismael had managed to secure. A handful of dried-out oak leaves, I now knew from where. More photographs of Chloe and myself, from the same collection as the one on their sideboard, and one of Mom, looking beautiful and radiant, on their wedding day. A letter from her, dated September 1923, shortly after she had received his letter, saying no more than *Thank you. I promise.* X. Some recent newspaper cuttings about The Roxy. And then, packed together tightly at the very bottom of the box, the collection of photographs that I knew to have been taken on that day by the dam, first mentioned to me by Gran and Grandad, and then regaled to me again by Ismael in more eloquent detail, a dreamy smile etched across his face as the familiar images flickered through his mind, like a silent movie. They were exactly as he had described, and more. It was all there to see, their close friendship, their joy and vitality, their sense of freedom and confidence, unconditional love and companionship. And so too their physical attraction and affection, rising three dimensionally out of the fleshy images with a carnal-like fervour that utterly dumbfounded me. There, before my very eyes, images of my father as a young man, handsome and majestic though he was, adorned in ostentatious role-play, wooing and goading his prey, like some music hall thespian. These were indeed the missing pieces of the puzzle that had so long eluded me and started to give meaning to the unsolved riddle, but they were bitter pills to swallow, if they were possible to countenance at all.

I had a sudden, visceral urge to distance myself

from it all, a feeling of total revulsion at the contents of the box and everything it stood for. I just wanted to get rid of the vile little thing and escape from this dastardly place, flee back to the security and comfort of my family, never to see these wretched people again. I felt tainted and tarnished, like they were trying to lure me into their disgusting lives, into their den of iniquity. It sickened me to think that this was my own flesh and blood, and I understood precisely why my mother reacted the way she had and wanted nothing more to do with him, with her, with it, with whatever Dad was. How dare they share these depraved images and curiosities with me and expect that it would miraculously wipe the slate clean, that I would simply welcome my father, or whoever he was, back into my life with open arms. What imbeciles! And a priest, at that! I regretted ever making the journey, ever knocking on that door and opening myself up to these two strangers, most of all agreeing to inspect the contents of this decrepit little box. It was all just so grotesque, and I wanted out, nothing more to do with it.

Seething, I packed my bags, checked out of the hotel and made for the car, and then, sitting in the driver's seat, ignition on, I suddenly remembered it, the box I had left on the table in the corner of the hotel bedroom, and Ismael's plea that I return it to him. Please, please, he had implored. Something brought me to my senses, some semblance of compassion buried deep down inside of me, triggered by his soft, gentle words describing the special memories that bound them together, their hope and strength for the future. No, I had to return it. I ran back into the hotel to save it from the cleaners and sure destruction.

Chapter 4

Father Mostert

District Six, Autumn 1968

Somehow, I knew we would not see him again. He had not taken the news well at all, and was unlikely to return. I never said as much to Ismael, but I am not sure I needed to – he had the same sense. I just hoped and prayed to God that he would return the box. Ismael would never have forgiven himself if he had lost it, the one thing that held such sentimental value to Alexis. What would he tell her? Fortunately, John had plucked up the courage to bring it back, although he asked one of the little kids in the street to drop it off at the house, long after the dust of his car had settled and he was well on his way back to the safety of his home, away from ours. Ismael's relief was palpable, and he vowed never to let the box out of his sight for as long as he lived, for as long as Alexis was by his side. Checking through its contents, he noticed a few additional items: photographs of John and his family, three lovely children, Alexis's grandchildren, standing together in front of the main house on the farm, as close and loving as any family could be, and a note addressed to Ismael and me, handwritten on hotel letterhead paper.

Dear Ismael and Father Mostert,

By the time you receive this note, I will be long gone. I am sorry that I did not come back to say goodbye, and hope that you have received the box back safely.

This has been very difficult for me, much more than I could have imagined. I will need time to digest everything and decide what to do next, if anything. Right now, it feels like our lives are best lived apart. I am all too aware that I never got to speak to ~~Alexis~~ Dad, but I would only ask that you please send him my love and wish him well, that is, if you even tell him about my visit. Maybe one day, we will meet again, but not now, I am sorry. Please take good care of him, and let me know if there is anything he needs, if I can help in any way.

Yours sincerely, his loving son, John.

We never told Alexis about his visit. It would have been too painful for her to hear that her son had struggled so much to understand and accept, that he had left without saying goodbye to anyone, before having the chance to meet with his father again, if ever. And the note, not even being able to acknowledge who she was, a line scratched through her name like a sword through the heart. It was not that she had any expectation that he would visit, none at all, but knowing that he had, that he had sat in her living room, metres away from the portrait with his sister, drinking tea and eating food from her crockery, sharing his deepest thoughts and emotions with Ismael and me, it would have been a bridge too far, or so we believed. The visit was best kept a secret, we resolved.

Ismael carefully replaced the photographs of John's family on top of their own, sealed up the box and returned it to its resting place, hidden as safely away as the visit itself. Ismael and I never heard from John again, not a peep. He disappeared from of our lives as suddenly as he had entered them. He was not about to reach out to Alexis, and so, to all intents and purposes, he returned to being no more than the young boy in the photograph on the sideboard, standing alongside his baby sister, their innocent little faces peering out into the world, oblivious to the voyage of discovery that lay ahead for them. He must have been overcome by shame and just decided he wanted nothing more to do with them, possibly even felt that he needed to protect his own family from the disgrace of it, from any possible scandal, and so it was easier to just forget and move on. Life in apartheid South Africa had enough challenges as it was, without something like this to contend with.

Ismael and Alexis received news from the farm periodically, via Ismael's younger sister, Yasmine, who still lived in the labourers' cottages and worked in the main house, as she had done her entire life, married now, with four children of her own. The news came through that Alexis's parents had died in quick succession of each other, as so many elderly couples do, the longing to be reunited on the other side outweighing the zest to begin a new chapter alone. The year was 1955, taking their innings well into their eighties, by which time management of the farm had become extremely demanding and draining for them. Overall, it had been a good innings, two lovely grandchildren, John and Chloe, five great-grandchildren who they saw regularly enough, and the enduring beauty and dynamism of the farm itself to invigorate them, right up to the end. Only the one disappointment to blot their landscape, the sudden departure of their son, wrenched away by forces of nature, with the finality of death.

They were the first people he had visited after Shirley threw him out, just a few possessions on the back seat of his car including the cause of his torment, that little box. He started to explain, but they beckoned him to remain silent. There was no need, they knew; they always had. They were so incredibly proud of what he had achieved, but they feared it would only be a question of time before this day would come. They had seen the love and kindness of Johan, they had witnessed their son's despair when he suddenly took off, and furtively, they had found and read his heart-breaking letter received after his passing. She had even worked out why her wardrobe kept shrinking, much to her considerable amusement. They had found the old copper plates capturing the images from that day in the attic, and curious as cats, re-processed them, smiles spreading across their faces and tears filling their eyes, as one picture after the next recreated the joy and happiness that their beloved son experienced that summer day in 1905. They loved him and accepted him for what he was, but they both knew that this would be their final farewell, the final hug, that they would never see their son again. He turned away from their long, warm embrace and made his way to the car, tears streaming down his face, looking back just once to smile and blow them a kiss, and then he was gone, leaving them standing on the porch all alone in the world. All alone, except for Yasmine, standing one step behind and above them, looking over their shoulders, as she had done all her life, their very own guardian angel.

As expected, John inherited the farm, but it posed a challenge for him, whether to change careers and move the family there, lock, stock and barrel, or attempt to juggle between the two. With the children still so young and in need of schooling, he chose the latter and moved freely between town and the farm, one day lawyer, one day farmer, all the time keeping the legacy of his grandparents on the farm alive. But it did not bring him the peace and happiness you would expect, so Yasmine detected. He would wander around the farm for hours on end, alone, head down, hands in pockets, kicking out at clumps of muddy grass, deep in thought, a sense of sadness about him. Occasionally, he would head off to the dam on the other side of the farm and spend the whole day there, only returning after dark, eyes red from the hay fever, he said, though she knew the look of an emotional and teary face when she saw one. She was aware of the little memorial he and his sister had erected in honour of their mother, but she always had the feeling that there was more to it than that, that these trips had more to do with the loss of his father and the unfinished business of his trip to District Six.

Sitting around the kitchen table late one evening, just before she was about to clock off for the night, he started to talk about faith and religion, and asked her what Islam taught about forgiveness, how it was possible for the true believer to repent for their sins. The discussion surprised her because she believed he had turned his back on religion, chosen the path of logic and fate, but she could see that he carried a load of guilt on his shoulders for which he wished to make amends, if only he knew how. She offered what advice she could, keeping it as generic as possible, without wanting to stray over the line of familiarity that divided a maid from her boss, but doubted whether it made much impact, such was the depth of his despair. She told Ismael about it, who in turn mentioned it to me, wondering whether John was perhaps experiencing some kind of road to Damascus, an awakening that would lead him back to Dover Street, or so Ismael hoped. He could not hide his disappointment when I said I thought not. I did not want to create false expectations, and I genuinely did not believe that John had it in him to retrace his steps and come face to face with the uncomfortable truth from which he had fled in such a cowardly fashion. Quite frankly, I did not believe he had it in him, the courage.

We are now in that fateful year, 1968. Still no news from John, other than the cursory update from Yasmine, but nothing of great significance. The eviction notices are coming thick and fast now, whole streets impacted at a time. The bulldozers have started their work on the outskirts of the District and are making their way inwards, yard by devastating yard. You can hear them, the angry growling of their engines, from which there is no escaping. People are having to pack up all of their belongings and move to their new tailor-made homes, thirty kilometres away on the windswept plains of the Cape Flats, a whole world away.

Nothing could have prepared them for the utter sense of loss and devastation, families, neighbourhoods and districts broken up and smashed apart. Never in my days as a pastor have I seen such pain and suffering, never have my services been in such need. Some simply cannot bear to watch it happen, and prefer to take matters into their own hands, their tragic souls rising above the malaise in search of a better place. Ismael was one such person. He had come to the end of his journey, his body riddled with the cancer and in excruciating pain for it. It was sad to have to say goodbye to my dear friend, and even sadder still to see Alexis by his bedside, saying hers. I prayed for them both, kissed him on the forehead and left them in peace to spend their final moments together. I looked back one last time at the two of them huddled together, and closing the door softly behind me, I headed back to the rectory to make an important phone call.

A month passed before Alexis received her notice, pinned to the door, like a nail to the cross. She told me she would like to sit it out to the end, and then make her way over to me at St Mark's when it was all done. It was almost as if she needed to see it for her own eyes to believe it, in the vain hope that this was all some terrible nightmare, that she would wake up in the morning and everything would be fine and dandy again. She had no plan that I was aware of, having rejected the place that had been allocated to her, and so I feared the worst, that she intended to follow in the footsteps of her dearly beloved Ismael.

I heard her footsteps clip-clopping slowly up the wooden floor of the church aisle towards the inside entrance of the rectory, echoing off the stone walls, as they always did, my early warning system of parishioners in need. Gingerly, she entered the living room, clutching her last remaining possession tightly under her arm, and made her way over to where I was standing. Without a word, she handed the box to me, together with a tightly folded piece of paper, and sat down. She looked utterly defeated and alone, like a child separated from its mother, not knowing where to go or what to do. I was at a complete loss what to say. After Ismael passed, I had called John and told him in no uncertain terms that the moment had arrived, that his father needed his help, it was time to come, urgently, before it was too late. But there was still no sign of him, not even a note, nothing. What could I do?

And then she spoke, looking at me directly in the eyes: "I know he came. I saw the photographs of the grandchildren in the box after he left. And I read the letter, 'Maybe, one day, we will meet again,' he had written. Well, I have been waiting for that day all my life, living in hope that he would pluck up the courage and visit me, just once."

She looked crest-fallen, at the end of the road.

My ears picked up the early warning signs of someone approaching from inside the nave, but hers didn't and she continued.

"But nothing, not so much as a word, not even condolences for the loss of my dear Izzy, only shame and embarrassment, it seems. Have I been so bad, has my life been so wrong, am I completely beyond redemption? I tried the best I could to do right by them, to make some small amends for all the pain I caused, I really did. I just hoped he would recognise it, just a little, and show to me, in some way, that he understood and that he does not hate me for it. Is this too much to ask, Mossie, please tell me?"

Before I could respond, I looked up and saw him standing in the doorway, eyes welled up, hands shaking visibly, looking a lot older than his age. The past fifteen years had not been kind to him, but he had finally come, thank God. He hesitated ever so slightly before making his way over to where she sat, and took her by the hand, helping her out of the chair. They stood looking at each other, holding hands, for what seemed like eternity, and then, without so much as a word, they wrapped their arms tightly around each other and stood hugging and sobbing until I worried they would suffocate one another, as if squeezing out the agony from the past so they could start afresh and be one again. I was moved to tears myself, knowing the journey each of them had taken to be here.

It was my cue to take my leave, give them the time and space they needed to start the process of healing and regenerating their relationship. But not before I heard her whisper, softly yet distinctly, "Oh, Johan, I missed you so much. I am so sorry, please forgive me." And his response: "No, please, I am the one who should be asking your forgiveness. It is I who have let you down. I am so very sorry, Mom." Johan and Alexis united in that moment.

It was dusk when I returned to the rectory. They were still there, huddled together under the lampshade, deep in conversation. There had been so much to catch up on. Tears had been replaced with laughter, burying a lifetime of sorrow and sadness. Their time had come, and they were making the most of it. Looking back on it now, I am not sure it could have happened in any other way. There will always be regret at the time lost, the missed opportunities to share important celebrations, to enjoy quality time with family, Ismael and Wendy in particular, the grandchildren too. But these paled into insignificance, when weighed against the miracle that they had been able to get together at all and reconnect in a way that neither of them could ever have dreamt of, and that I was privileged to have witnessed that day.

Johan insisted that she come back to the farm with him and spend the rest of her days in its familiar surroundings and in the company of close family. In doing so, he underestimated how far Alexis had travelled into her new world and away from the old. Everything had changed, much more even than her sexual identity. She had been reclassified, officially, from white to coloured, so that she could live with Ismael in a coloured-denoted suburb, as required by the new suite of apartheid laws. It meant sitting in different pews in church, entering the non-white entrance in the post office, travelling in the upstairs seats on buses, standing back in mandated deference for white people to pass, carrying the correct identification papers in fear of arrest, avoiding the glare of a police officer, and everything that rendered a person of colour second class, the sacrifices that Alexis made in order to be true to herself, to be who and what she was. It also meant fresh friends, different places, new ceremonies, alternative activities, all of which she eagerly embraced, elements of the happy life shared with Ismael, which made the sacrifice so worthwhile.

But the sad reality of her new world was that it had been blown to smithereens and no longer existed, something she had not fully grasped as yet, even as her home lay freshly demolished and she sat, homeless, in my living room. This was my moment. I took her by the hand and led her onto the little porch at the side of the church that overlooked what was left of District Six. I pointed in the direction of Hanover Street, its buildings lying on the ground like a row of broken teeth.

"Look, look at what they have done. It is all gone and can never be the same again. Listen to Johan, there is no more life to be had here. Your place is on the farm now, it beckons you back. Hear its call."

Tears streamed down my face as I presided over the impromptu memorial of our dearly beloved neighbourhood, and I realised that my words rang as true for all the souls who had called this place their home, echoing off the mountain and across the city bowl for everyone to hear, if only someone would listen, anyone. It was a life-defining moment for all three of us, the realisation that a chapter had been shut tight and that a new one must begin.

I have never felt so alone as the moment I watched Johan drive off with my dear friend perched in the passenger seat of his car, the box resting on her lap, her little white handkerchief waving me goodbye out the window for the last time. Alone, but happy, happy for them.

The Farm, Autumn 1970

We are at the farm, assembled under the oak trees lining the banks of the dam. I am administering the last rights in accordance with Alexis's wishes, her last will and testament. The whole family is here, John, his wife Wendy and their three children, Chloe, her husband Peter and their two children, down from Johannesburg, and alongside them, still rooted in the ground, the memorial to Shirley, without whom the family would not be. Yasmine and her husband, Yusuf, are there too, though not their children, which everyone understands. John and Chloe's children, the grandchildren, are all in their late teens and early twenties, roughly the same age as Alexis, Johan and Ismael when they met for the first time, here on the farm, all those years ago, in 1905. They rose at daybreak and made their way to the dam, armed only with a trowel, to prepare the final resting place, an earthy tomb where the three urns will be laid side by side, Alexis in the middle, as decreed. The oak trees whispered knowingly amongst themselves when they spotted the little troupe make its way across the grassy fields towards them. They must prepare to bear witness one more time.

There has been much discussion about the box, whether it should be buried with the three urns to accompany them on their journey into the afterlife, as was the practice of pharaohs, or whether it should be conserved in a place of safekeeping for the benefit of the living. Quite apart from the spiritual aspect, the question has a practical angle to it – how big the burial pit needs to be. There are two opposing points of view, fuelled by the ambiguity of the note that Alexis handed to me at St Mark's the morning after her home had been demolished, her last will and testament:

> *Inside this box are two sets of ashes. Please place mine with them and bury us together under the oak trees along the wall of the dam.*

No one had thought to clarify the meaning of these words while she was alive. It seemed insensitive and unimportant to do so. Now, it seemed inconsiderate not to have asked, and of utmost importance to know so as to ensure her last wishes could be respected. Alexis had treasured the box and kept it by her side throughout the trials and tribulations of her life as a source of comfort and strength, a reminder of the past and a beacon of light for the future. She told me how she had plucked up the courage to unseal the lid the night before the bulldozers came, sitting alone in her living room, awaiting her fate. Her hands had indeed trembled in the anticipation of it, releasing a lifetime of memories and taking her back to those early days on the farm with Johan, to see his young face once again, to run through the fields with him, to swim in the dam, lie on the grass, tickle his feet, stroke his hair, caress his skin and make love in the shade of the oak trees, their own special place, a celebration of their dream together. The lock of hair, still soft and smooth, was a painful reminder that this was not to be, their fate etched in the withered oak leaves lining the box, motioning Alexis on and away from the farm towards pastures new, new places, new faces, a long and winding road to the eventual peace and quiet of Dover Street and her adoring Ismael. Pandora's box indeed, though not all evil, much goodness there too, no question.

They had not yet resolved the matter at the time of digging, and so they dug a hole large enough to accommodate the box in the event that that was their final verdict.

Bury it, and it will be at the mercy of the maggots, forever forgotten, never again to enchant, beguile, comfort and guide. Safekeep it, and it will stand forever as a monument to hope and truth and love. I knew what my choice would be.

My eulogy cannot possibly do justice to what has gone before, but something must be said.

"We are burying three people this day, all of them for the first time, in a place that is sacred to them. Together in life, they found the freedom to be who and what they were, to be truthful to themselves and to each other, to look past their differences and to accept and love each other unconditionally.

They were the lucky ones in a way, lucky to have experienced harmony between raw nature and human life, a bridge that few of us have dared to walk, even if we knew how. The farm provided them with a sanctuary to mould their glorious universe, free from the pressures and prejudices that ravage our country, but they had the courage of their convictions to step out of their hiding and sprinkle their stardust wherever they ventured. Their road was surely a lonely one as each one of them was required to turn their backs on everything they had and everyone they loved, sometimes more than once, leaving behind broken hearts and unfulfilled dreams. Such is the lot of the trailblazer. They were ahead of their time, without knowing it and without deriving any benefit from it. In fact, they paid the ultimate sacrifice of never witnessing the fruits of their bravery, as so many adventurers before them. We were the ones who had to play catch, or lose. We were the ones who had to learn and understand where they were headed, and follow. We still are. We pay tribute to them for who and for what they were, and for the light they shine on others like them, for us all."

I wanted this to be about the three of them, not about us, not about politics and the pain that surrounds it. And I wanted it to be as much for the future generation standing around our little burial chamber looking forward as it was for the present generation looking back.

I am about to bring the proceedings to a close, when Johan takes a step forward and begins to speak, looking up into the canopy of trees enveloping us, as a cathedral.

"Alexis brought me to this spot when I was a child, when she was my father. She told me how special it had been to her, that it was the place where Chloe and I had first been conceived, and she dedicated it to us, calling it our sacred place. When our dear mother Shirley died, we innocently attributed that honour to her, and through this small memorial, consecrated the place to her. I told Alexis about this just a few months ago. She was greatly amused that Chloe and I assumed we had been physically conceived here, but she understood only too well why we had jumped to this conclusion. She was deeply touched that we had thought to dedicate this spot to our mother, recognising the huge sacrifices she made in bringing us up and never betraying her loyalty to Alex, tempting though that undoubtedly had been over her lifetime. Alexis asked me to bring her back to the riverbank one last time so that she could pay her last respects to Shirley."

Johan pauses, casts his eyes down the bank towards the water glistening in the background, then continues.

"It had been forty-eight years since we last visited the place together, but it seemed like the day before. Everything was exactly as it had been, only more beautiful and peaceful than I remembered. We stood in silence, side by side, staring down at the little memorial, thoughts racing around our heads, no words needed. It was a moment to cherish, somehow spiritual, this last goodbye, this last token of our appreciation to the true heroine of this saga, our vigil to Mom. Time passed. Alexis took me by the hand and led me a few steps away to where we were facing down the wall of the dam, across its tranquil waters and over to the grass swaying in the afternoon breeze. Then she said: 'This *is* the place where you and Chloe were first conceived, where I lay with Johan, staring up at the sky and dreaming of the family we would never have, tearful at the thought of it. It was the moment we both realised how futile we truly were, that our dream could never be more than fantasy, and it marked the beginning of our end, as sure as a death knell. It was as exhilarating as it was tragic, the absolute pinnacle of my life. I have never felt such love and such loss, all at once, as I did that afternoon. You and Chloe were not just a miracle of God, but you are the living embodiment of that love and of that loss.'"

John pauses again, reaches into his pocket and pulls out a lock of bright blond hair, freshly shampooed and glistening in the sun, like a nugget of gold. He clasps his hand around it and continues. "And it came to me, in that moment, for the first time in my lifelong search for the truth. God has blessed me with no less than two mothers, two beautiful, loving, caring human beings, and a father, someone I only ever knew from fables and photographs, but someone who was nonetheless as real and as dutiful as any, the tall, handsome young man who arrived unannounced at the farm all those years ago, my father, Johan."

A gust of wind blows up from across the dam and rustles through the trees, leaves fluttering around us like confetti. I know they are together again.

About the Author

Anthony Sauerman was born in Cape Town and lived the first thirty years of his life there before moving to the United Kingdom in 1995. There he practised law as an in-house lawyer in the life sciences industry before retiring in 2020 to take up his passion for writing. Since then, he has published two books related to the work he did during his legal career and *The Box*, which is his first foray into fiction writing.

He currently lives in London with his husband, Manfred, who he met in Cape Town thirty years ago.

Printed in Great Britain
by Amazon

31552860R00061